PUF~~~~

THE ABSO~~~~
ADVENTURES O~ ~~~DREAMER DEV

Ken Spillman developed his imagination while playing games in bushland, on the edge of one of Australia's most isolated cities, and by reading adventures set in faraway places. He is now the author of around eighty books, published in around twenty languages. Ken is a frequent visitor to India and has written a number of books featuring sharp-witted young Indian characters. These include the Daydreamer Dev stories; *Advaita the Writer* (2011); *No Fear, Jiyaa!* (2017); and *Radhika Takes the Plunge* (2012), which was listed in *101 Indian Children's Books We Love!* For more information, visit www.kenspillman.com.

PRAISE FOR THE BOOK

'Ken Spillman knows all about kids. He frequently gets in their heads and comes up with the most imaginative and creative results' —*The Star*

'[Spillman] paints his characters with warmth and sympathy, sketching just enough of their fine details to lift them beyond the typical caricatures of much writing for young people'—*West Australian*

'Spillman knows how to capture children and their quirks and everyday experiences with an honesty that will have both adults and kids nodding and smiling'—*Kids' Book Review*

'If there were just one reason why writers should be treasured, it is that they can articulate the inarticulate. That's exactly what Spillman does'—*Sunday Times Magazine*

The ABSOLUTELY TRUE ADVENTURES of DAYDREAMER DEV

KEN SPILLMAN

ILLUSTRATIONS BY MICHELLE FAROOQI

PUFFIN BOOKS

An imprint of Penguin Random House

PUFFIN BOOKS

USA | Canada | UK | Ireland | Australia
New Zealand | India | South Africa | China

Puffin Books is part of the Penguin Random House group of companies
whose addresses can be found at global.penguinrandomhouse.com

Published by Penguin Random House India Pvt. Ltd
7th Floor, Infinity Tower C, DLF Cyber City,
Gurgaon 122 002, Haryana, India

Penguin
Random House
India

This omnibus edition published in Puffin Books by
Penguin Random House India 2019

Daydreamer Dev Climbs Mount Everest was first published in Puffin Books
by Penguin Random House India 2011

Daydreamer Dev Traces the Amazon was first published in Puffin Books
by Penguin Random House India 2011

Daydreamer Dev Crosses the Sahara was first published in Puffin Books
by Penguin Random House India 2012

Text copyright © Ken Spillman 2011, 2012
Illustration copyright © Michelle Farooqi 2011, 2012

All rights reserved

10 9 8 7 6 5 4 3 2

ISBN 9780143449782

Printed at Replika Press Pvt. Ltd, India

www.penguin.co.in

MIX
Paper from
responsible sources
FSC® C016779

CONTENTS

INTRODUCTION

Before my first visit to India more than a dozen years ago, I was advised by several compatriots that I would either love it, and plan to return, or find it an interesting eye-opener to be filed under 'once-only experiences'. India has changed much since then— as have I—but I knew within twenty-four hours that I would be back. My regular visits to India now account for well over one year of my life. I have countless Indian friends and, for my reading, I choose Indian fiction over that of any other country.

I had never planned to write stories with Indian characters and settings, and the first one came to me while I was writing something else. That first story was about a homesick girl in love with reading and inspired by Ruskin Bond, and I just had to give it priority. Later published as *Advaita the Writer*, it paved the way for many more books set in India or featuring Indian characters living in Australia.

As I reflect on this now, I see just how inspired I have been—and how *immediately* inspired I was—by the spirit of India. My characters are inclined to take on life's challenges with imagination and a sense of humour. They are optimistic, enterprising, feisty and unbreakable. These are attributes I associate more with the people of India than those of any other country, and perhaps the 'no-limits' attitude underpinning the reveries of Dev is my central message to all young readers.

The Daydreamer Dev stories were first published in separate volumes, and each of those has been out of print for a number of years now. I am delighted, therefore, to be able to bring all three to a new young readership in this special omnibus edition. I trust that Dev's journeys will bring you all the fun and adventure I experienced while travelling by his side.

The stories were written for every kid who has ever taken an extraordinary flight of fancy because, as Albert Einstein once said, 'Imagination is more important than knowledge. For knowledge is limited, whereas imagination embraces the entire world'.

—KS

DAYDREAMER DEV CLIMBS MOUNT EVEREST

DEDICATED TO ARJUN VAJPAI

and to those who allow young people to dream

1.

Baba had two favourite subjects. The first was the superiority of the carpets sold at Kwality Carpets. Baba's *other* favourite subject made

Dev want to plop himself down on one of those high quality carpets and fly away.

Sometimes, that is exactly what he did— and who could say that he didn't?

Off he would go, high above the noise of Delhi, up through the dust and smog to a place of . . .

What? Other wonderful things, other imaginings!

He didn't tell Baba of his travels. He didn't even tell Baba of his thoughts.

He couldn't.

He couldn't because Baba's *other* favourite subject was daydreaming. The importance of *not* daydreaming, to be precise. The importance of *Dev* not daydreaming, to be still more precise.

'It is unfortunate for you,' Baba lectured, 'that there are no

Ken Spillman

prizes for daydreaming. You would be top of the class! All India champion!'

Dev liked that idea. To become a champion would be awesome—without having to lift a single finger! Perhaps he could even go to the Olympics and win gold. He would stand with tears in his upturned eyes, mouthing the words

of the national anthem 'Jana Gana Mana' as the
tricolour ascended the flagpole.

Bhārata bhāgya vidhāta
Jaya he jaya he jaya he
Jaya jaya jaya jaya he!

Baba's morning lectures followed his night-time lectures. Night lectures followed notes sent home from school, and notes from school followed lectures from Mrs Kaur.

The pattern had such familiarity. Mrs
Kaur's notes were so regularly in Dev's satchel
that Amma only rolled her eyes as she fished
them out.

'That woman should photocopy one of
these notes,' she said once. 'Then she could
sign and date it only.'

Dev smiled. He liked Mrs Kaur, in spite of her notes.

'Oh Dev!' Amma said. 'What shall we do with you?'

2.

Dev kissed Amma and went down two flights of stairs to the shop. Baba sat at his cluttered desk, pressing buttons on a calculator.

'You see this?' Baba said, pointing to the calculator. 'This does not daydream. It lives by the truth of numbers! And this month, the numbers are not so dreamy.'

'I'm sorry, Baba.'

'No more notes, Dev. Please listen in class. How can you learn if you don't listen?'

Dev didn't know.

As he made his way to school, he saw OP kicking a bottle cap along the side of the road.

'Wait!' he called.

OP kicked the bottle cap into the traffic and watched it dance and dodge and clip the wheels of cars, motorbikes and autos.

'Dude,' he said as Dev reached him. 'That maths homework was hard!'

Dev groaned. He hadn't even known where to start. Baba's calculator lived by the truth of numbers, but Mrs Kaur's homework held their secrets. Dev wished again to be like the kids who unlocked such secrets without effort. He wished again that he pleased Mrs Kaur more often.

OP didn't like numbers either. What OP liked was facts that hardly anybody else knew. He collected them like others collect foreign coins. A lull in any conversation was all it took

Ken Spillman

for OP to rummage through his collection and gleefully produce a shiny fact.

'Did you know that a Chinese dude bounced a football on his head 341 times in sixty seconds?'

Dev scoffed. 'What? You're joking!'

'And did you know that a sixteen-year-old dude from Noida climbed Mount Everest?'

Dev didn't. His mouth dropped open.

'Yes, yes!' OP exclaimed, his eyes alight. 'Arjun Vajpai did it—8,848 metres above sea level!'

Eight thousand, eight hundred and forty-eight metres? What a view! From that height, Mrs Kaur's maths homework and those notes that upset Baba and Amma would look small.

Very small.

Lucky Arjun! Dev thought.

3.

All through the morning's Hindi and General
Knowledge lessons, Dev listened with fierce
concentration. He coloured his map of India
carefully, never allowing the pencil to cross
state borders.

After lunch, Mrs Kaur began her science
lesson. Dev felt hot and drowsy. Mrs Kaur
opened the windows and turned on the
overhead fans.

Pht-pht-pht they went. Outside, the traffic
hummed and honked.

Pht-pht-pht went the fans. *Pht-pht-pht*.

Chka-chka-chka went the helicopter's blades above Dev's head.

He felt a bitter chill.

Chka-chka-chka. Light snow fell. With his school satchel over his shoulder, Dev clung to the rope and was lowered to the ground. A cluster of tents was abuzz with satellite phones.

Journalists rushed back and forth between them.

'At last,' Dev thought. 'Base camp.'

'He's arrived,' said a man dressed in so many layers of clothing that he looked the size of a sumo wrestler.

In the shadow of Mount Everest, Dev was surrounded by a small welcoming throng. Questions came at him thick and fast.

'Why Everest? Isn't maths challenging you enough?'

'Were you inspired by Arjun?'

'How old are you, Dev?' This came from
a woman with an American accent. 'Where
are your parents? Where is your jacket? Why
attempt this alone, without oxygen?'

Dev wanted only to get on with his climb.
There was no time for such questions.

'Oxygen tanks are heavy, no?' he said. 'I
would rather take this!'

He tapped his school satchel, opened it and, to his surprise, saw a chocolate bar. He held it up, then put it away quickly as he felt his mouth water.

A couple of journalists scribbled on their pads. Others talked into little machines.

'A chocolate bar! How wonderful! But you will catch a terrible cold wearing only that school uniform!'

'When do you plan to set out?' asked another.

'Right now,' Dev said. 'The summit awaits!'

4.

'Wait!'

The voice came from a Sherpa woman,
shimmering behind the flames of a campfire.
She wore high boots, long woollen pantaloons
and a coarse robe, with a sash around the
middle. Perched on her head was a colourful
bonnet.

'Auntie, I must go.'

'You do not know the way,' said the
woman.

'The way? Of course I know the way.'

The woman looked at him doubtfully. 'And it is . . .'

Surely she was trying to make a fool of him. Dev laughed. '*Up*, of course!'

Everybody knew that. The summit of Everest? How much further up was it possible to go without wings, or a rug from Kwality Carpets? The woman eyed Dev thoughtfully.

'Correct—up! But there are many ways one can go up, and none of them are easy.'

'Auntie, you are very kind, but I'm quite a climber you know. For many years I have climbed banyan trees and eucalyptus. And I have also climbed to the roof of Kwality Carpets— that is best when Baba is angry with me. Please point out the *shortest* way and I will go.'

'I will come with you.'

'But Auntie, you are not so young.'

'And you are *so* young. I am a Sherpa. I have climbed Everest to the summit. I died coming down and now live without fear, hunger or age.'

'Coo-ool,' Dev said in wonder. Somehow he hadn't expected to meet a ghost—but if the Sherpa really *was* a ghost, he'd still be climbing solo, no? 'Okay, come,' he said. 'But let's hurry!'

'We must first ask for the mountain's blessing,' she replied.

This they did. Then Sherpa Auntie gathered up a rucksack, and off they went.

5.

'We have reached Icefall,' Sherpa Auntie said.

White cliff faces and peaks surrounded
them, but Dev couldn't see anything falling.

'Icefall?' He questioned, puffing hard. It had
already been a long climb. 'Are we near the top?'

'Oh no. . . But we cannot get there
without first passing Icefall, and here many die.
A heavy lump of ice might fall on you. A crack
might open up and swallow you. Here, ice and
snow and rocks tumble down in a great rush
almost every day.'

'Like an avalanche?'

Sherpa Auntie nodded.

Dev had seen avalanches on TV, and he didn't have to wait long to see one for real. The sound came first, a distant whooshing and rumbling. High above, ice boulders had suddenly broken free. They were tumbling down the mountain as if hurled by an angry giant.

'*Quick!*' Sherpa Auntie cried. She grabbed

the strap of Dev's satchel and almost tugged his arm out from its socket as she drew him behind a big wall of ice.

Dev flattened himself against it. Truckloads of white rubble crashed over their heads. Lying on a railway track with a train passing could not have been more terrifying—but Dev felt nothing but the thrill of adventure.

'Cool!' he said.

'You were lucky,' said the woman.

'Sherpa Auntie, don't you mean that *we* were lucky?'

'I'm already dead, remember? It's not so easy to die twice. Once bitten, twice shy!'

'Auntie, did you *really* die?'

'Oh yes,' she replied. 'Mercifully, it was quick. Now, give thanks to the mountain for sparing you.'

Dev smiled broadly. He faced the ice wall again, placed his hands together and bowed his head.

'I have a feeling you are only being cheeky,'

Sherpa Auntie told him. 'Everest has no time for smart alecks.'

They set off again. At the foot of an even larger wall of ice, the woman opened her rucksack and took out two ice picks and an

assortment of climbing gear. She laid them out carefully, and looked up the sheer ice face.

'Follow me,' she said. 'Don't lose your grip on the rope, but climb with your legs, okay?'

Dev wanted to say, 'I'll go first,' but thought better of it.

6.

The higher they climbed, the harder it got.
At the top of the ice wall, Dev sat down,
exhausted.

'If you stay like that, your bottom will
freeze and stick hard to the ice.'

'Auntie, if that happened I would get pizza
delivery by rescue helicopter. I would melt the
ice with the force of nature.'

Sherpa Auntie chuckled, and Dev got up
to face the next part of the climb. As they
passed through the Valley of Silence, there was

scarcely one moment of silence. Ice cracking deep in the glacier sent murmurings into the biting air, while Sherpa Auntie kept Dev entertained with her stories.

'My name is Pasang Lhamu Sherpa—you can Google me. I was the first woman to summit this mountain. Going up went well—going down was the death of me.'

'Auntie, why not just sit on something and slide down? Next time, I will bring you a rug from Kwality Carpets. On a nice blue one I even flew to the moon and landed softly. Today I will empty my satchel and ride it like a sled.'

'So full of ideas! Good for you. Some will work, some will not. That one will not.'

A little further on, Pasang spoke of Tenzing Norgay. 'Oh yes, that first time with Edmund Hillary he summited exactly as a baby climbs into the lap of its mother. That is what he told me—and that is what Everest is to us—Mother of the World. I also knew Babu—he climbed seven times without oxygen!'

Ken Spillman

'Auntie, how long have you been a Sherpa?'

'That, young man, is a most ridiculous question. One doesn't *become* a Sherpa—one is *born* a Sherpa, just as the Queen of England is *born* English.'

Well, thought Dev, *if I had the choice between being born a Sherpa and the Queen of England, I'd give up the throne in a flash!*

Ken Spillman

7.

'There are no plants here, Sherpa Auntie,' Dev said. Rocks now peeped through the ice and snow, and the view behind them was stunning. Clouds rolled in across the lower ranges of the Himalayas.

'Plants are more sensible than people,' Sherpa Auntie replied. 'They grow where they grow.'

Dev thought for a while. The air was thin. He felt heavy and was breathing short and fast. 'But will I not grow if I strive for new heights?'

'Ah,' sighed the woman. 'Now you are talking about the mind, and the spirit. And those are different. There you will grow.'

Dev knew she was right. He already felt respect for the mountain. In its size there was majesty, and in its majesty there was a beauty that even the Taj Mahal couldn't match.

They came upon a long, flat stretch and the going was easier—until the heavens unleased a snowfall and high winds forced Dev to lean sideways like a speed skater on a turn.

'A blizzard,' Sherpa Auntie grumbled. 'This is what comes when you ask for blessing without sincerity.'

Dev stayed silent, watching the snow thicken on the ground. He knew he'd been too cocky, and prayed for the Mother of the World's forgiveness. For a while, she refused. Dev was bashed around the ears by sleet, and he longed for one of Sherpa Auntie's strange caps. He ploughed through cushions of snow, uncertain whether he should have undertaken the journey at all.

Dev tried to breathe deeply, but felt like he was hardly breathing at all.

What this place needs, he thought, *is more air. Why don't they pump some up from below?*

'Lhotse Wall,' said Sherpa Auntie, pointing. A steep, icy incline lay before them. Was it harder or easier than the last? Dev didn't know or care—he just needed the strength to climb it.

8.

Dev felt dizzy.

Is that why people say 'dizzy heights'? He wondered. But Lhotse Wall was now behind them, the summit nearer.

Sherpa Auntie kept a steady pace and Dev struggled to keep up. His school satchel weighed more than a set of encyclopaedia. If not for the chocolate bar, he would have cast it into the void—but how would he explain that to Amma?

Dev followed Sherpa Auntie around ledges

and across slippery platforms of rock and ice. After another sheer climb she halted, waiting for him.

'Do you know what place we will now enter?' she asked.

'A good place, I hope. A place where escalators and elevators take us directly to the summit.'

Sherpa Auntie smiled. 'There is not much to be gained by convenience. We are entering the Death Zone.'

'*Fine*,' said Dev. 'That isn't the place I had in mind. But Auntie, I must eat first. My jaw won't have movement if I don't use it any longer, and my stomach's drilling through me.'

Dev unbuckled his satchel and fished inside for the chocolate bar. His frostbitten fingers struggled with the wrapper, but eventually broke through. He eyed the chocolate hungrily, then glanced at Sherpa Auntie. With effort, he snapped it in two and offered her half.

'You are a good boy. But I hunger for nothing and watch my waistline—there's no weight like dead weight.'

Dev grinned, cracking his parched lips. He crunched at the frozen chocolate, and slowly it thawed in his mouth. He barely tasted it.

He didn't want to ask how the Death Zone got its name.

He didn't have to.

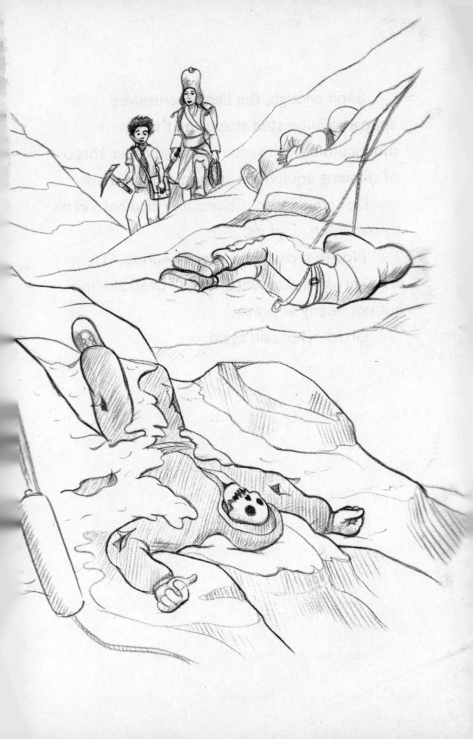

Soon enough, the dead themselves appeared in twisted shapes on the mountainside, with old ropes and other shreds of climbing equipment strewn around them.

Dev shuddered. Chocolatey acid rose in his throat. 'Ohh. . . *gross!*'

'Not so gross,' said Sherpa Auntie. 'They are sherpas and mountaineers—dead like me but not nearly as pretty.'

'Gross,' Dev said again.

9.

The plateau looked familiar—like photographs he'd seen of the surface of the moon. The sky had cleared and was deep, deep blue. Dev could see the wide tan plains of Tibet. He thought no more of the dead. Each step seemed one beyond his limit.

Perhaps, Dev thought, *this IS the moon. Perhaps I fell asleep at Kwality Carpets and sailed into space.* Yes, that was it—outer space on planet Earth. Somewhere below, the people of every nation lived and breathed.

Dev *longed* to breathe. Gasping, he heard Sherpa Auntie urging him on but could say nothing in reply. He also longed to pee—but how could he tell the woman to wait if his voice had frozen up?

Dev remembered something he had read: 'The power of the mind is limitless.' He repeated it over and over, silently. He was determined to reach the summit, determined to hold in his pee until he did.

Sherpa Auntie announced locations like a tour guide. Dev saw their destination now and felt an unexpected surge of energy. Then, Sherpa Auntie led him through a deep furrow to another sharp slope. His heart sank.

'Knife Ridge and the Hillary Step,' Sherpa Auntie said.

The ridge looked deadly, so steep that it blocked his view to the summit.

Halfway up, the snow gave way and Dev slid back, almost losing his ice pick. Crazy with exhaustion, he abandoned himself to the

Ken Spillman

possibility of slipping and bouncing all the way back to base camp. But a hidden rock caught him, and Sherpa Auntie called him on.

The famous peak—seen always from afar—was nowhere to be seen. Dev topped rise after rise, driven only by hope.

'Almost there,' Sherpa Auntie told him.

She was right. At the next glorious crest, a downward slope greeted them. Sherpa Auntie put down her rucksack, triumphant. For Dev, relief came first.

Finally, he thought.

Then joy thawed him, took hold of him. Remembering the miraculous appearance of the chocolate bar, Dev felt in his satchel for a flag. There it was—the tricolour! He wrapped himself in it and stood on top of the world, the curve of the earth's surface visible in every direction.

'You made it,' Sherpa Auntie nodded. 'But remember this—most accidents happen on the descent. You cannot afford to relax.'

'I made it,' Dev said, finding his voice. *Now*, he thought, *I must pee.*

Sherpa Auntie caught his eye. 'Dev, a test is a test. Give each part your full attention, or you will surely fail.'

10.

Mrs Kaur stood in front of him. OP's pencil was scratching feverishly at the desk beside him. Dev's test paper was untouched, but he felt fantastic.

'Dev,' Mrs Kaur said. 'A test is a test. Give each part your full attention, or you will surely fail.'

Pht-pht-pht went the fans. *Pht-pht-pht.*

OP looked up. 'Dev has a very bad headache, Mrs Kaur. He cannot concentrate. Even at lunch time he was telling me this.'

'Is that true, Dev?'

Dev nodded grimly. 'It is true, Mrs Kaur. But also I must use the washroom. Please, Mrs Kaur, it is urgent.'

When Dev returned, OP lifted his eyes, pursed his lips and shook his head.

I saved you, OP was saying. Dev beamed at him and Mrs Kaur noticed. She beckoned.

'Your head feels better, I see. Is it connected with your bladder? There was a cure for you in the washroom?'

'Mrs Kaur . . .'

'A sick boy does not smile like that, Dev.'

'Mrs Kaur, every bone in my body is aching but I have much to smile about.'

His teacher studied him. Her lips formed a question, but left it unsaid. Instead, she opened the drawer and took out her notepaper.

'I will write to inform your parents that I detained you after school to complete today's science test. I do not know where this will end, Dev. Your behaviour in class is not the behaviour of a boy who wants to go up in the world, is it?'

'Mrs Kaur, I am sorry. But there are many ways one can go up, no?'

DAYDREAMER DEV TRACES THE AMAZON

DEDICATED TO THE PEOPLE OF
PROJECT AMAZONAS

*a non-political, non-sectarian organization working to
serve the people of the Amazon and conserve the rainforest*

1.

Dev heard OP tapping on the front window of the shop. Kwality Carpets was not yet open for business—but OP wanted to see Dev, not

Baba's carpets. It was Sunday, the best day of the week.

Upstairs, Baba was still applying a fine-toothed comb to Dev's mid-term report. He had begun yesterday afternoon and then launched into a lecture at dinner. With Amma insisting on Dev's regular bedtime, the conclusion had been postponed. Baba was not one to leave things incomplete.

'*Dev is a capable student who must be more attentive in class and apply himself consistently.* What do you think Mrs Kaur means by that? Listening, not your useless daydreaming!'

Finally Baba stood up. OP was still tapping on the glass downstairs, and Dev raced down the stairs eager to escape. A day free from the classroom gaze of Mrs Kaur stretched in front of him.

It was already uncomfortably hot outside, but Dev draped an arm over OP's shoulder as they passed still-sleepy vendors. At the slum, the bare feet of toddlers were treading on

ground that would soon burn the hooves of cows. Down on the hard, flat riverbed, boys were playing cricket. The river's tree-lined banks provided dense shade, like Nature's AC.

'In Australia, some rivers *never* run,' OP stated, making himself comfortable. 'After heavy rains there is water, but not enough to flow.' OP's brain was crammed with facts. Most were useless but he stored them anyway, as if all facts were equal.

'Those are not rivers,' Dev reasoned. 'Those are puddles.'

'Australians exaggerate, so they call them rivers.'

'Our mighty Ganga, that is a river. It is the longest, no?'

'It is not—but the longest river depends on

where you start measuring. Some say the Nile, some the Amazon. But the Amazon is the mightiest. One fifth of all the water in all the rivers of the world belongs to the Ama . . .'

A ball shot past, narrowly missing Dev's head. Laughing, OP retrieved it and scampered down to the riverbed, signalling six in a comic fashion before flinging the ball back. An older boy instructed him to stay there as a fielder, and despite the heat he didn't protest.

Dev climbed a tree and leaned back in one of its forks. There was the faintest puff of hot breeze, and leaves rustled around him.

Dev closed his eyes.

2.

'Where am I?'

The sound of motorcycles and auto rickshaws was familiar, but the air was dank and the sky a brilliant blue.

Dev climbed down from his tree. A brass band struck up as his feet touched the ground, and a man at the head of a welcoming party extended a hand.

'Welcome to Iquitos,' said the man. 'My name is Salomón Arraya, and I am the mayor. We are honoured that you have chosen our city to commence your Amazon journey.'

'Even I am honoured,' replied Dev. 'I did not choose Iquitos—Iquitos chose me.'

'Such eloquence!' Señor Arraya exclaimed. 'Good fellow, it is no wonder you achieve such great things.'

'Tell me about your city,' said Dev. 'Surely it is the finest city in all . . .'

'Peru,' said Señor Arraya helpfully. 'Indeed it is! We have many old mansions—one of them designed by Señor Eiffel. His tower in Paris you may have seen?'

Dev hadn't, but nodded as if he'd been there only yesterday.

'We have four universities. We also host an important research organization, Project Amazonas, and a field laboratory that catalogues species of animals and plants, discovering new ones . . .'

'Cool,' said Dev. 'But maybe I should, er . . . find the river?'

'As you wish,' said Señor Arraya. 'Follow me.'

The band struck up again, marching them

past a giant cathedral and the town square to a little quay on a wide expanse of water. An aluminium boat garlanded with lilies awaited Dev. A gleaming engine idled lazily behind it.

'Behold the Amazon!' Señor Arraya announced triumphantly, silencing the band.

'So this is where the river starts?'

The mayor smiled. 'Who can say? We are just downstream from the Ucayali and Marañón, the Amazon's two main tributaries. For us it

starts here. It also ends here, depending on the direction one travels.'

Dev clambered on board the boat. The mayor signalled to the bandmaster, who raised his baton grandly.

'*Buen viaje*,' said Señor Arraya.

The band played. Señor Arraya produced a sword, slashed the boat's tether and sent Dev on his way.

3.

With the Iquitos quay becoming more distant, Dev heard the music stop and felt suddenly alone.

He worked to master the bar that controlled the rudder, and carefully adjusted the throttle. It was similar to the one on Baba's motorcycle, and soon he was beyond the city in waters lined by jungle. A variety of river vessels passed, many with cargoes of timber.

Dev was sure that tracing the Amazon couldn't be difficult, but the mayoral reception had distracted him from the task at hand. Now, questions fired from one part of his brain bombarded another.

What if he was totally embarrassing himself by heading upstream?

Did the food cooler he could see in the bow of the boat hold provisions? Did it contain chocolates?

Would he have enough fuel? Could he complete the journey and get back to Kwality Carpets before dinner?

Dev slowed the vessel and studied the water, looking for signs of a current. A small branch floating near the boat reassured him— until he saw its eyes.

Alligator, Dev thought, breathless.

It wasn't nearly as big as some of the alligators he'd seen on TV, but he didn't fancy being the one to tell it. He steered the boat away, avoiding sharp movement. The reptile might only be big enough to eat half of him, but that was one half too much.

Ken Spillman

Taking the boat closer to the shore, Dev heard monkeys feeding in the jungle canopy. The litter they dropped fell directly into the river, and Dev watched it carefully.

Phew, he thought. *I'm going with the flow.*

4.

Eventually night fell. The stars were bright and the mosquitoes hungry. Dev wondered what time it was back home, and how much longer the journey would take. It would end on the coast of Brazil—but how far was that?

In daylight he had been able to see sloth-like jungle creatures and huge, colourful birds, but in darkness his adventure seemed less exotic.

If I wanted to get eaten by mosquitoes, I could stay home and wait for the monsoon, Dev thought.

He decided to put the engine on full throttle to see what the little boat was capable

of. At high speed, perhaps, the mosquitoes would leave him alone.

Instantly, the engine roared. Dev was almost thrown overboard as the boat zoomed off, its nose in the air and a trail of froth behind it. His heart pumped.

Awesome! Dev stood up in the boat, the wind tossing his air and the steering bar clenched between his knees.

He yelled into the night. 'Yee-ha! Next stop the coast!'

CRR-ACK!

Dev's next thought was about piranhas. He found himself catapulted into the air, with the boat cartwheeling beside him.

Next stop? Murky water.

When Dev surfaced, all was silent. The boat was overturned. Keel up, it was floating away.

'Hey kiddo!'

It was a man's voice, quite close by.

'Don't go feeling sorry for yourself. Spare a thought for that giant turtle you hit. She's like a hundred years old and was only just coming out of her shell. Now you've gone and used her for a speed bump!'

Forgetting all about piranhas, Dev scanned the river's edge.

'Over here,' called the man.

He was sitting on a log, fifteen metres away. Even in the moonlight Dev could see that he was a big guy, with a fair complexion and a strong, bare chest.

'Need some help?'

Dev thought that much was obvious. The man plunged into the water and disappeared, surfacing finally near the boat. He flipped it over almost effortlessly, then climbed in and unfastened the oars. He manoeuvred the boat towards Dev.

'Hold on and I'll get us over to shore,' he said, extending an oar. 'We'll need to check this baby out.'

'I thought Tarzan lived in Africa,' sputtered Dev.

'Don't insult me,' the man replied. 'Tarzan was a man. I'm a *legend*.'

5.

'Are you one of those scientists who count species, or what?'

Dev sat dripping on a small mud bank between the jungle and the river as the man inspected his boat.

'I told you, kiddo, I'm a legend.'

Well, thought Dev, *he's seriously strong, but that's no reason to have such a high opinion of himself.*

'I can guess what you're thinking, kiddo, but it's true—I'm an actual legend. I could've told you I'm a dolphin, but right now I don't look like one.'

Dev wasn't sure what to say. Clearly this dude was mad. Dev only hoped he wasn't dangerous.

'I'm a pink river dolphin, to be precise. Around these parts, the locals call me a *boto*.'

I bet they do, thought Dev. *Where I come from, they'd call you a lunatic.*

'And if you want to know, I'm rare and endangered.'

Ken Spillman

'Oh right! I'm sorry to hear it.'

Humour him, Dev thought. *Then he won't be expecting it if I need to hit him over the head with an oar.*

'According to legend, a *boto* can transform into a handsome young man at night. They say we go ashore to chase girls, but that part's wrong. It's got nothing to do with girls, kiddo—it's just because we can! If you guys could turn into dolphins and swim, you'd do it right?'

The *boto* was right. Dev could picture himself leaping high out of the water and entertaining tourists, just for the joy of it.

'You're a lucky kid—your boat's okay,' the *boto* announced. 'I'll just get the engine turning over and you'll be off. And by the way, that's a tarantula giving you the eyeball . . .'

Beside Dev, there was a spider bigger than the *boto*'s hand and with more hair than Baba's legs. Dev edged away, watching it carefully.

'Those babies eat birds for breakfast,' said the *boto*. 'Come on, I'll join you and be your river guide till it's time for me to freak you out and swap these arms for fins.'

6.

'I'm not like other dolphins,' the *boto* said.

After starting the engine, he had steered the boat just far enough from the riverside to avoid fallen branches.

'That is obvious,' Dev said. 'First, you're talking to me. Second, you look more like an Olympic swimmer.'

'Hey that's insult *numero duo*, kiddo— watch yourself. Those swimmers are *slow!* But here's the reason I'm one cool dolphin. Being a *boto* means I'm the only kind of dolphin—get that? The *only* kind—with neck

movement. I can turn my head from side to side.'

Somehow Dev had never thought of any dolphins as being disabled, but he could see that the *boto* had a point. A neck that actually *moved* definitely seemed to be an advantage.

'But enough about me. Since you also turn your head from side to side, you ought to do it more often. This is the Amazon, kiddo—it's no place for blinkers!'

'What do you mean?'

'Well, you could miss an alligator, or a caiman . . .'

'A what?'

'A caiman. Like an alligator only smaller—a stumpy-nosed thing.'

'I think I already saw one,' said Dev. 'First I thought it was a branch.'

'That's the one, kiddo. Caimans just *love* acting like branches—not the most entertaining guys in the Amazon.'

With the *boto* at the helm, the boat sped

through the night. Dev noticed that he didn't seem worried about turtles, but knew the *boto* understood the river and probably had better night vision. Time passed quickly.

'Are we still in Peru?'

'You're joking, kiddo. We left Leticia way back!'

'Who?'

The *boto* laughed. 'Leticia's a *place*, kind of—a piece of Colombia where Peru meets Brazil. Couple of years ago, some poor tribe got busted there. Lived happily for millennia, not needing the rest of the world, then bang! Someone finds them and they're famous.'

'So we're in Brazil?'

'Bra-seeel. World's fifth largest country. Land of coffee, football and samba. Enjoy!'

7.

Hours later, the boat passed through a large city.

'This is Manaus,' the *boto* announced.

The air was heavy, not only with moisture but also with woodsmoke and the smell of cooking. Dev realized he was famished. With all the excitement of the journey and his brushes with the caiman, the giant turtle and the tarantula—not to mention his strange friend, the *boto*—he had completely forgotten about the provisions from Iquitos.

As he unclipped the top of the waterproof

cooler, Dev's eyes lit up. A chocolate bar!
It lay between three bananas and a foil-
wrapped package.

Dev pocketed the chocolate bar and
unwrapped the package. It contained thin strips
of red meat, so hard and dry that they might
have been leather. Dev almost vomited.

The *boto* chuckled. 'It's called jerky—dried

beef. The American tourists I meet go crazy for that stuff.'

Dev couldn't imagine anything worse. He re-wrapped it and dropped it back into the cooler. For now, it had even put him off the chocolate.

'Speaking of food,' the *boto* said, 'I could eat about ten big piranhas right now.'

Dev shuddered.

'I'm serious, kiddo! They're like my favourite food! Hmmm, piraanhaaa . . .'

'More like you'd be *their* favourite food,' Dev said.

'What you guys don't get is that most piranhas are vegetarian . . .'

'Veg? No way! That's coo-ool . . . they're like me!'

'Piranhas get false criticism because of a minority, you know? But those red-bellied non-veg types *do* tend to get nasty when they're hungry. They strip meat right to the bone.'

Dev had seen non-veg *people* do exactly the same thing.

'But let's not talk about my breakfast,' the *boto* said. 'It's still a while until morning.'

'Would piranhas eat that jerky stuff?'

'Sure, if they're non-veg . . .'

Dev cast out the contents of the foil. The jerky had barely landed before the water turned into a vortex of frenzied fangs.

'I guess those guys aren't veg,' Dev remarked, awestruck.

8.

The river had become wider. Even above the noise of the engine, far from the riverbank, Dev could hear the restless jungle. The darkness was lifting. Birds cawed and screeched, impatient for the day.

'Kiddo, the time has come.'

Dev knew what the *boto* meant. He still found it difficult to believe the dolphin story, but regardless of that he wanted the *boto*'s company right down to the river mouth. Who knows what might have happened if he hadn't been around when the boat flipped? Even if

he wasn't a legend, he sure was a good guy to have on board.

But the *boto* was obviously intent on leaving. He shook Dev's hand. 'It's been a pleasure,' he said. 'Give my regards to the señoritas on the coast and your folks back home.'

With that, he leapt off the boat. Dev watched bubbles rise where the *boto* had landed, but there was no sign of him. Then, ahead of the boat, a large dolphin leapt high from the water. Almost white against the dawn sky, it spun its head left and right before arcing into the water.

'Show off,' muttered Dev, smiling.

With the disappearance of the *boto*, Dev felt overcome with exhaustion. He unwrapped

his chocolate bar and devoured it in two bites. Then, one by one, he ate the bananas, chewing them slowly to pass the time, struggling to stay awake.

The coast, surely, would arrive soon. If he switched off the engine to rest for a while, he would drift. The river knew its course.

Dev stretched out in the boat and fell asleep.

9.

When Dev awoke, the sun was high and his boat was stationary, lodged under a low branch overhanging the water.

He was sharing it with an anaconda.

Green and ink-blotched, it was gigantic. Though part of it was still wrapped around the branch, there was a heavy coil near Dev's feet and a large head near his elbow. Sunlight shimmered on its skin.

Dev was panic-stricken, unable to move. Even if he *could* move, what should he do? Staying where he was would invite the

anaconda to crush and swallow him—slowly.
If he jumped overboard, he'd probably make
some non-veg piranhas extremely happy. Using
the branch to get ashore seemed Dev's only
chance.

He summoned his courage and, very slowly,
lifted his head.

The anaconda also lifted its head.

Dev lowered his head.

The snake studied him for a moment, then lowered its head too.

Dev jumped up, the boat rocking wildly.

The anaconda reared and struck, seizing Dev's upper arm. It gripped him tight—so tight that Dev let out a word that Baba sometimes used, and which Amma didn't like.

Dev grabbed at the snake, desperately trying to free himself. He could feel its muscles rippling beneath the smooth scales. *This is it,* he thought. A loop of anaconda was rising from the deck, ready to squeeze the life out of him.

Instinctively, Dev sank his teeth into the snake's sinewy neck. The anaconda jolted and seethed, but refused to let go. Monkeys were watching the show, screeching and applauding. Birds squawked as if they cared. Dev bit harder.

At that moment, there was a terrific crash. The boat lurched, coming free of the branch under the weight of a third combatant—a dolphin that had launched itself from the water. Chirruping hysterically, it was now imposing its bulk on the reptile's coils.

Dev felt the jaws of the snake release him. He too released the snake, but only to punch it mightily on the nose. Probably unaccustomed to being bitten and boxed— and certainly distracted by the spectacle of the dolphin—the anaconda retreated to its branch. With that, the dolphin heaved itself up and dropped daintily overboard, setting the boat adrift.

Dev started up the engine. The dolphin

Ken Spillman

sculled around the boat, still chirruping, turning its head left and right above the water.

'Okay I get it,' Dev laughed. 'You're a legend!'

He saluted the *boto*, rotated the throttle and made for the coast.

10.

'Yes, I'm a legend,' OP was saying. 'Everyone saw my catch except you. I wasn't even watching and the ball flew at me so fast—no time to think! The human brain has 100 billion cells and can send messages at a speed of 120 metres per second. Luckily there's only one metre between my brain and my hand, so I had enough time . . .'

'OP, I made it.'

'What?'

'To the coast. The *boto* saved me and when I got there, people were cheering . . .'

'Oh yes, they were cheering me! Everyone
except you! I can't *bee-lieeve* you missed my
catch. My *first* and *only* catch! There are twenty-
seven bones in each hand and a complex
network of muscles. Everything worked
perfectly, Dev—I'm a legend.'

Dev climbed down from the tree and put
his arm around his friend.

'Sorry, OP, I was somewhere else. Next

time you're going to do something amazing, just tell me, okay?'

OP smiled. 'I'm starving,' he said. 'Let's go eat—we haven't had anything all day.'

Dev didn't want to mention the chocolate bar. 'Maybe Ajay Uncle will give us some peanuts,' he suggested.

As they walked, Dev rubbed a throbbing pain in his arm and considered the day's adventure.

'OP, I've been wondering,' Dev said. 'What do you know about Amazon wildlife?'

DAYDREAMER DEV
CROSSES THE SAHARA

DEDICATED TO JOHN HARE

Whose account of his Sahara crossing greatly assisted me, and more importantly raised awareness about Asia's critically endangered twin-humped Bactrian camels.

1.

Dev shrank into the huge chair. If he was to list ten places he'd like to be in, in exact order of preference, this one would be *tenth*.

Mr Bannerji was a nice man but he was a headmaster, nonetheless. He sat on the other side of a vast desk, his long fingers restlessly entangled like a nest of snakes. Mrs Kaur, Dev's class teacher, sat demurely to Dev's right. Baba had plonked himself on Dev's left after handing the headmaster a Kwality Carpets visiting card and promising attractive discounts.

Mr Bannerji cleared his throat. 'We think Dev is a fine boy,' he began, looking directly at Baba. 'And we do not doubt his academic capabilities. We are only concerned about one thing: his ability to concentrate.'

Baba squirmed. Every day, he reminded Dev to pay attention, apply unceasing effort, and—above all—curb his daydreaming.

Ken Spillman

After smiling kindly at Dev, Mr Bannerji turned back to Baba. 'There may be certain *conditions*, shall we say, that would reward investigation.'

'Are you referring to . . . a dis*order*?' Baba gritted his teeth, relaxing only to give undue emphasis to 'order'. For a moment, Dev thought Baba had said 'odour'.

'Perhaps,' nodded Mr Bannerji. 'But Dev is passing all tests with good marks and this is not a matter of life and death, so to speak. We only alert you to possibilities because we sincerely believe Dev can go far.'

'Sir, I am most grateful for your concern and will consider your advice carefully. At the

same time, I must respectfully ask that you apply strict discipline.' Here, Baba rose up, puffed his chest and raised a finger. 'After all, how is it that Dev can be allowed to occupy his own world for hours—in a *classroom?*'

Mrs Kaur opened her mouth, ready to defend her methods. Mr Bannerji cut her short.

'Rest assured,' he said, 'we attend to the individual needs of our students at all times.'

The meeting was over. Mr Bannerji ushered them to the door. He shook Baba's hand, patted Dev on the shoulder and called for his next appointment.

Dev knew Baba, and he knew what was coming next.

It began with the letter L.

2.

Oh, how Dev loved lectures! He delighted in Baba's eloquence, admired his endurance. He only hoped he might one day be *half* as excellent.

In fact, just a *quarter* would do. Or one-hundredth.

Then again, perhaps Dev wouldn't lecture anyone at all. Ever. Yes, that's what he'd choose. To tell the truth, he wished his father possessed less enthusiasm and stamina.

Mr Bannerji had said that he could go far. Far was where Dev always wanted to go. Perhaps he could go even now—to the red

heart of Australia or the icy wastes of the
North Pole.

Anywhere.

By now, Baba was in full flow. 'I built
Kwality Carpets from the ground up. Did I do
that by daydreaming?'

Miserable as he was, Dev had an urge to smile. He had flown 'from the ground up' on rugs from Kwality Carpets so many times, off to adventures far from home and lectures. Baba didn't know about that, though perhaps he wouldn't care. Baba only cared about school.

'And now you have Mr Bannerji thinking there is something *wrong* with you. Where will this end, Dev?'

Dev wished he knew.

Mr Bannerji's words rolled around in his head.

Far. He *would* go far! One day he would be a grey-haired prime minister, with his friend OP as his top adviser. In the meantime, while his hair was still black, he'd win a medal at the Olympics, swim across oceans, fly solo around the world. Maybe he would even cross the Sahara.

Nothing could be as difficult as reaching Kwality Carpets and walking upstairs

Ken Spillman

without collapsing under the weight of Baba's words.

When they finally arrived, Dev went straight to the roof, stretched out on his favourite old rug and gazed into the clouds. He let them wrap him in a cocoon. The clouds drifted.

Dev drifted too.

3.

'Dude, finally!'

OP was sitting on the rail of a fence, waiting for him. Behind him, camels shuffled

in the dust inside their pen, heads held high.
A camel trader squatted in the shade of a
makeshift shelter, his turban wrapped like a
bandage. Not far away, shimmering in the heat,
Dev saw a sandstone mosque, a network
of ancient bungalows, and a few stunted
acacia trees.

'I've been here for hours,' OP
complained, 'and if you know anything about
Timbuktu, that isn't good.'

OP was one person who knew the facts
about any place. Dev was sure his friend knew

more facts than anyone, and also that OP liked nothing better than sharing them.

'It's Baba's fault,' Dev said simply.

'We need dromedaries,' OP told him. 'Six—two each and two for our supplies.'

'What's a dromedary? And *what* supplies?'

OP pointed to a stack of chaff bags, rice sacks, and waterbags, together with a small cooler. Dev nodded in approval.

'See those camels? They're dromedaries,' OP said.

Dev ignored him, now more interested in something else. 'What's inside the cooler?'

'Mangoes and chocolate bars,' smiled OP. 'But here's the bad news. That trader dude wants half the mangoes and *all* the chocolate bars in exchange for his camels. Prices are high in Timbuktu.'

'Do we actually *need* two camels each?'

'*Dromedaries,* dude. They're tough, but it's backup.'

'We will haggle. We can take our chances with five, and keep a couple of chocolate bars each.'

OP considered this, and then nodded. 'It's a risk, but so is crossing the Sahara with a guy who has never heard of a dromedary. Let's do it!'

4.

Dev didn't know how to choose camels,
but warned OP against taking any that came
recommended by the old trader.

'He will take us for fools and offload the
worst of them,' Dev argued. 'Let's look at their
teeth—that's how they choose horses on TV.'

Dev gestured to a camel and peeled back
his own lips to show the turbaned trader what
he wanted him to do.

The old man smiled in a devilish manner,
but did what he was asked.

The camel's breath stank, and the animal
made matters worse by belching in Dev's face.

'Phoo-ee!' Dev exclaimed, jumping back.

OP held his nose and walked away in disgust. 'We're not taking *that* one.'

But the other camels weren't any better. A municipal water tanker full of mouthwash wouldn't have been enough to make their breath decent. They chewed their cud, swallowed it and regurgitated it again. They spent every minute of their lives becoming more smelly.

Finally the boys made their choices, taking the three biggest camels and the only two that were patterned in brown and white.

'Brown and white camels,' said Dev. 'Are those rare?'

'Skewbald *dromedaries*,' OP corrected. 'I must admit I didn't know they existed.'

The trader seemed to be indicating that the two skewbalds were deaf, but the boys couldn't see how that mattered.

'I'm guessing they wouldn't understand English or Hindi anyway,' laughed Dev.

5.

Camels plodded—that's what they did. Dev
could walk just as fast himself. The only fun
part so far had been when his camel stood up,
making him lurch violently back, and almost as
suddenly forward. Dev wished they could sell
the animals and get motorbikes instead.

The camel train's lazy pace was only one
of his irritations. Another was the persistence
of flies, attracted by the moisture on his skin
and in his eyes. Worse, Dev had made a big
mistake by allowing OP to mount the leading
camel. He'd thought *nothing* could smell
worse than a camel's breath, but as much as

they burped and belched, the emissions from the opposite end were worse. OP's camel alone was letting out enough greenhouse gas to finish off the ozone layer, without any assistance from fossil fuels. But now, there was no escape.

'I am telling you, when we get to an oasis we will swap places,' Dev said.

OP must have heard, but any reply was lost in the vast expanse ahead. Left to his own thoughts, Dev wondered where they'd started from. Timbuktu, OP had said—but that wasn't a *real* place, was it?

'Hey!' This time, Dev shouted.

OP twisted and sat backwards on his camel to face Dev.

'What *was* that place back there?'

'Timbuktu. It's in Mali.'

'*Really?* And that's in the Sahara Desert?'

'It isn't,' admitted OP. 'But it's close. And by the way—just say the *Sahara*. That means desert, so Sahara Desert actually means Desert Desert.' At this he laughed, hoisted his legs up and spun round again.

There was plenty of sand around them, but no rolling dunes. The ground was rocky, dotted with giant termite mounds. Dev even saw goats in the scrub, herded by boys among small, whitish bushes.

The camel's gait rocked him back and forth. Dev began to relax, closing his eyes like a baby in the arms of a particularly stinky

mother. Now and then he was disturbed by the skewbald camels behind him, prone to sudden jitters as if phantom sounds intruded on the silence of their world.

This would be a long journey—but now that Dev thought about it, he was in no hurry to get home.

Ken Spillman

6.

The dunes came soon enough. They traversed one, skirted another. Sand rippled under the camels' strange cloven feet. Sometimes, they sank hock deep but the beasts strode on, grunting and groaning. The boys had finished their mangoes, with the last droplets of juice consumed by flies. Swirling sand had by now filled their hair, scratched their eyes and stuck to their skin.

A speck on the horizon divided into two as they got closer. These then became camels with another speck sitting on one. OP twisted round, anxious.

'Dude, trouble. I've read of bandits roaming these parts.'

Dev had a fleeting vision of himself offering a chocolate bar in exchange for his life—but what would stop a *real* villain from taking both?

'What can we do?' he asked.

'Not much,' OP replied. 'Hope?'

They ploughed on and before long the seated speck took on the shape of a man

in robes. He wore a huge turban, and Dev couldn't help thinking that he resembled Aladdin's genie.

The man smiled at them broadly. 'You are too young,' he adjudged, as if that was funny.

'You speak English?' Dev asked, surprised.

'I am speaking eight languages. Most you do not know. Where you go?' The man eyed their camels with interest.

'We are crossing the Sahara from the south,' OP replied proudly.

'My young friend, you cross only from fool to dead fool. This wrong way. You very lucky you find Ibrahim. I come. Later, give me your sons of donkeys. Okay, deal?'

'These are dromedaries,' OP said, offended. He wasn't used to being called a fool. He tapped his compass twice, but wasn't in a position to quarrel. Besides, what use would their animals be at journey's end?

Ibrahim linked his camels to OP's and off they went.

Dev smirked. Now OP too would be surrounded by air thick with camel gas.

7.

Dev's confidence in OP's navigation skills had been shaken. He now put his faith in Ibrahim, who in turn put his faith in Allah.

Listening to Ibrahim, it would be easy to think his second most powerful belief was his own infallibility. Resting at a scraggy oasis, he sipped sugary green tea and rated himself the best Saharan guide, the finest judge of camels, and master of the largest domed tent. But there was something in his eagerness to impress that made Dev pity him.

'I am indeed the greatest of all Tuaregs,' Ibrahim claimed, perhaps trying to convince himself.

'What's a Tuareg?' Dev asked OP later. Ibrahim was snoring and the boys had decided to celebrate his disinterest in robbery by eating their chocolate bars. 'A kind of car? Something from Star Wars?'

'A tribe—a nomadic tribe. Ibrahim should know the Sahara backwards.'

Another time, Ibrahim talked about *amana*.

'A *what*?'

Ken Spillman

Ibrahim appeared delighted by Dev's ignorance. 'A-ma-na. Man trust camel, is *amana!* Trust—like bank!'

But from what Dev had heard Baba say, some banks didn't deserve *amana.* Camels? Maybe. Dev had certainly learned that you could trust them to smell bad and make you saddle-sore.

The days were as hot as home, and Dev's lips cracked and bled. Temperatures plummeted at night and he slept fitfully. He huddled inside a supply bag emptied of chaff by the camels, which only made him itchy as well as cold. The sand looked soft but was like a bed of stone. Dev rose at each glowing dawn like an imitation of his grandfather.

On they went. There was barely any fodder left for the camels. *What use is* amana *if the miserable creatures are starving?* Dev wondered. He was almost in the same state himself. Rationing the small amount of water

seemed to have shrivelled every cell in his body. Camel skeletons protruded from the sand. Oases were few and far between.

'You need more oases,' Dev told Ibrahim desperately. 'People should dig wells, plant trees . . .'

Smiling, Ibrahim cut him off. 'Allah want more? Then Allah give water, not give Sahara.'

Ken Spillman

He was right. Dev knew that the Sahara wouldn't be the Sahara if it was one big oasis.

OP calculated that he was swaying on his camels at a rate of four thousand times per hour.

Dev calculated that OP was seriously affected by the sun if he thought *that* was even worth calculating.

8.

Dev was flagging, but OP was flagging even
more. One of his eyes was inflamed, and he was
extremely irritable. He was outraged to find
that Ibrahim was leading them toward Algiers,
not Tripoli as he had planned. He repeated
'dromedary' like a chant and was even riled by
the word 'dunes', insisting that great oceans
of sand were known as '*ergs*'. This Ibrahim
confirmed, but they then argued over the status
of the Sahara as the world's biggest desert.

'A desert is judged by rainfall,' OP
contended. 'Antarctica is the largest low rainfall
area. The Sahara is second!'

Ibrahim scoffed, but Dev saw that he was hurt. He may not have heard of Antarctica, but that didn't stop him from cursing OP in eight different languages.

Occasionally they crossed dusty roads, but none of them went where Ibrahim wanted to go. The softer the ground, the more empty the horizon, the more relaxed he seemed. He subsisted on a pocketful of dates, sometimes nibbling on one and returning it to his pocket. He rarely sipped from his flask, and would not touch the boys' supplies.

Whirlwinds rose up from nowhere. Some collapsed, only to regroup and lash the camel train with sand-laden fury. As each wild wind veered and teetered away, Dev imagined it laughing.

OP became feverish. One day, just before nightfall, Ibrahim looked closely at his eye.

'I will cut,' he declared. 'Or your friend will not see his children.'

Horrified as Dev was, he suspected Ibrahim was right. A layer of tissue had grown across a tiny cluster of sand particles on the surface of OP's eye. OP had no way of seeing it for himself, but he knew that for all Ibrahim's ignorance about Antarctica, a Tuareg *should* understand problems caused by sand.

Ibrahim produced a razor blade

from a leather sheath. Dev shuddered and turned away.

'Dev,' said OP, 'you do it.'

'No way. You are delirious.'

'Dude, he strokes his dromedaries as if their filthy coats are fine silk sarees. He picks their teeth and their noses, he wipes their eyes. His fingernails are blacker than Mr Bannerji's shoes. You must do it. Please.'

Ibrahim handed Dev the razor blade and threw up his hands. 'Blind fool,' he spat. He walked over to his camels and caressed one exaggeratedly.

The very thought of taking a razor to OP's bloodshot eye made Dev sick, but he knelt and examined the filmy membrane. The lump was clearly visible beneath it. Dev steeled himself, knowing what he had to do. He looked at OP, brave and trusting.

Amana, he thought.

Carefully, he slit the membrane. A slimy ball of sand slid free. Dev had not drawn blood.

'Don't move,' he said. 'Rest.'

OP blinked both eyes and Dev stood up.
He exhaled the breath he'd been holding in.
He listened beyond the snorting of one restless
skewbald and immersed himself in the silence
of the desert. He had a feeling that things
would now be fine.

Ken Spillman

9.

'Keep those sons of donkeys,' Ibrahim
huffed, and then refused to speak to them.
Gone was his cheer. Completely dispirited,
Ibrahim even stopped talking to himself.

But OP was feeling better, and they
had left the great *ergs* behind. The camels
plodded across stony fields, pausing at times to
wrap their elastic mouths around dry grass or
stunted bushes.

Seeing a jagged horizon, Dev called to
OP: 'Are those mountains?'

'Probably,' OP told him. 'Part of the Atlas
range, I guess. That's exactly why I was going

north-east to Tripoli, not *due* north to Algiers. The mountains drop off as they run east. Don't blame me, blame Ibrahim.'

Dev didn't want to blame anyone. He'd had more than enough of the Sahara, and surely reaching the mountains meant they'd succeeded in crossing it? Rock-strewn trails

through the mountains promised a refreshing
change. As long as the camels could last out, he
would too.

Amana, he thought again. *Believe*.

Near a village at the foot of the
mountains, the camels gorged themselves on
succulent acacia. The Berber villagers spoke

to Ibrahim in Arabic. Soon there was music, an ensemble of women pounding goatskin drums. Men, women and children danced to greet the travellers.

While a feast was being prepared, Ibrahim approached the boys. He ignored OP and addressed Dev.

'I eat, take food for camels, I go. Yes, I take your sons of donkeys. Three only. I give you those that do not hear. Take other guide from here.'

Dev felt another pang of sympathy for him. Ibrahim unhitched the two skewbald camels and prepared to depart after the feast. OP watched guiltily.

'Ibrahim,' he said, bowing slightly. 'You helped two Indian boys do what none have done before. Your knowledge saved my eye. You are the most brilliant guide, the finest of Tuaregs.'

'I am,' agreed Ibrahim, standing taller.

'And I am sorry for my rudeness,'
continued OP. 'I had lost my mind.'

Now Ibrahim's smile returned, and he
looked every bit a genie. 'Yes,' he grinned. 'You
did. Now we eat.'

10.

OP was beside Dev with a packet of *kachoris*.

'Let's eat,' he said, thrusting it at Dev. 'They're still hot.'

'The weather too,' Dev moaned, sitting up. His back and buttocks were sore, in spite of the rug under him. Lying on the roof of Kwality Carpets, the sun had burned his face. He hadn't cried after Baba's lecture, but his eyes felt sticky.

Dev sucked at the dry air. 'Where did you get these?'

'Amma. Again she took me to the doctor. So worried she has been. I am always tired and my eye has been sore for quite some time.'

Now Dev saw the redness in one of OP's eyes. He nibbled at his treat. 'What did the doctor say?'

'Eye is fine. But I must rest.'

'That makes two of us. I'm exhausted,' Dev said. 'And by the way, OP, you owe me.'

'I owe you? You are one crazy dude. It's me who brought you *kachoris*! But guess what? Amma bought me a new atlas.'

'That reminds me. I want to ask you something. Have you ever heard of the Atlas Mountains?'

ACKNOWLEDGEMENTS

I could not have documented these chronicles of Daydreamer Dev's restless imagination without the support of a small group of very special people.

Jaya Bhattacharji Rose was a wonderful sounding board as I embarked on the first Dev journey; since that time, I have been fortunate to work with three excellent editors—Sohini Mitra, Amrita Mukerji and Shalini Agrawal.

In particular, I express deep gratitude to Sohini, who has had cause to be cranky with me but never been anything but patient, generous and receptive. The respect I developed for Sohini as my editor more than seven years ago has grown steadily through the vicissitudes of my writing life, and I am thankful that our association continues.

Thanks also to Sangeeta Bhansali, who helped the original Daydreamer Dev books reach underprivileged children served by NGOs; Gaurav Jain, for believing; and finally, to Michelle Farooqi, whose illustrations capture the life of Dev's adventures.

—KS